Let's Hide in the Castle

By David Evans

Table of Contents

Chapter One: The Start of Everything

During the worldwide zombie outbreak, Loraine and Douglas were on the run in London. They had to leave there home behind due to the constant zombie attacks that happened in their neighborhood. The first week of the outbreak, the Police were avidly patrolling the streets. A man had transformed into a zombie and ambushed one of the Police officers biting him on his arm and soon afterwards he turned into a zombie.

He slowly lumbered along moaning with blood running out of his mouth, and his eyes were blood shot. He kept on wandering down the street of the neighborhood growling and moaning. People were utterly terrified of him and stayed locked inside their homes. There was one man outside, cutting the grass not paying attention to anything.

Once he saw a zombie he stopped what he was doing and ran down the narrow street towards the town. He left the lawn mower idling not caring about it what's so ever. He ran for his life, but he tripped over the man hole cover and landed flat on his face. He was dazed and confused for a good couple of minutes, and once he felt better he tried to stand up but had a hard time.

He must have strained his ankle and he could barely put any pressure on it. The zombie came lumbering along and saw him lying on the ground, the zombie immediately ran up on him and bit him on his throat. Blood came gushing out of his throat, he couldn't breath and his eyes rolled back in his head and he stopped breathing. The zombie continued on to consume him, he bit into his arm and ripped it from his dead body. The man was eaten by the zombie, a few minutes the dead man came alive and began to lumber on down the street. Day after grueling day more people were becoming infected.

The people who worked in the Pet Shop were the last people in the town to get infected by the unknown virus. The people in the Pet Shop watched in horror how a large crowd of zombies lumbered along past them. Luckily the window in the front of the pet shop was reinforced with plexiglass.

There were several employees trapped inside of the Animal Clinic. They were all terrified for their lives, a women screamed when she saw a zombie next to the window.

There was blood coming out of his eyes and mouth, he let out a faint growl. He kept on pushing forcefully up against the window, soon the rest of the zombies followed suit and eventually the window couldn't withstand the force and fell in.

The people in the Animal Clinic couldn't seem to get the back door opened, it was jammed. The one man in the back of the shop was so scared that he fell down and soon after passed out.

The other people were trying relentlessly to get out. Finally, they were able to get the back door open, it was still too late. The zombies overtook the store in just minutes. Everyone in the Animal Clinic got bit and now were infected. Everyone in the town was infected except for two. There were now crowds of zombies wondering around aimlessly in the middle of the streets. Some zombies were slamming up against cars and attacking each other, one zombie ripped the other zombies arm off and began to feed on it. After just two days the Police Department was over taken too.

The officers had guns, but they weren't powerful, the zombies were able to take over. One of the officers had a shotgun and unloaded all the bullets on the zombies as they broke into the Police Station, but still was no use. There wasn't much that could be done, zombies were all over the place.

There were no longer no places to hide from them in the town, Meanwhile at the Naval Submarine Base in Kings Bay, chaos broke out after the enraged zombies breached one of the two entrance barriers. The sailors began firing into the crowds of zombies from up in the guard towers, while the Commander had the mission on his mind.

He happened to look out the window and saw a zombie going after one of the sailors, he immediately grabbed his pistol and frantically ran out of his office. He began opening fire on the zombie, hitting it in the abdomen then the head. He could see the sheer panic in the sailors eyes, and looked him over for any bites.

"Did you get bitten anywhere?"

"No."

"What happened to your gun?"

"I lended it to the guard."

You could have gotten yourself killed, you obviously weren't thinking clearly. We'll discuss your disciplinary matters later, the sailor saluted him. Hold on don't go away yet, I haven't saw the guard dog and I'd like if you would go look for him. I don't feel comfortable with doing that, especially with the zombies running around.

Since you're not going to look for the dog then board the submarine and get it ready to go. Don't give me any excuses, you know what needs to be done and the sailor walked away. The Commander went back into his office and got on the loudspeaker, attention sailors I want you to stop what you're doing and listen to me.

We must board the vessels immediately, the zombies are close to breaking through the 2nd barrier. We can't afford to defend this base much longer, so everyone get a move on. A concerned sailor entered the room, with the look of fear in his eyes. Sir we have a big problem, several sailors have been bitten.

"Where are those sailors now?"

"Standing behind the second barriers."

I would tell you to go get them, but it isn't worth the risk. Allow me to escort you to the submarine, but the other sailors they'll be coming right behind you don't worry. I'm going to miss the guard dog, don't cut to conclusions. He's probably lost around here somewhere, I would like if he would come with us in the submarine. I've been meaning to ask you something, I always ask you because you always know most answers. You go ahead of me, the sailor carefully climbed down into the submarine. The Commander took out his mini binoculars, excuse me Commander we have to get past you, you're blocking our way.

Sorry about that, I wasn't paying attention to anyone around me. Eventually the last sailor boarded the submarine, the Commander was keeping an eye on the second barrier. The guard dog came out of nowhere and came running over to him, I'm so glad to see you.

The dog promptly sat down next to him, and he gently petted him on the head. His cell phone began to ring, so he took it out of his pocket and answered the call. Hello this is Commander Larnell from the Naval Submarine Base in New London, we had to leave our base because it was overtaken by vicious zombies.

Ten of my sailors were killed by the zombies, and to make matters worse some of my vessels were attacked by an enemy vessel, one of our light attack submarines were destroyed by the enemy.

"Is there any chance that we can meet at sea?"

"Yes."

I just don't like telling you certain things over the phone, that's understandable. Suddenly he heard the phone drop, and there was nothing but silence. Then the Commander picked up again and was out of breath, I just don't know what we're going to do. You won't believe what's going on in this vessel, two of my sailors have transformed into zombies and we had to lock them in the engine room.

I can't believe what a disaster it has become, eventually we were able to lock on to the enemy vessel and blow it up. I hope that you never go through what I'm going through right now.

"What kind of ship was the enemy vessel?"

"A destroyer"

"Why didn't you shoot the zombies?"

Because they're my own men and I don't want to harm them. This sailor just won't get away from me, he's trying to bite me. Then hang up the phone and shoot him, that's when the phone went silent once again and he would never hear from him again.

He quickly put his phone away and brought up his binoculars again, and this time he noticed that the second barrier had been breached and the zombies we're coming his way now.

He quickly climbed down into the submarine, and his dog followed him and one of the sailors closed the hatch and they were on their way. The Commander retreated back to his quarters, where he was greeted by one of the sailors.

"How long is this mission going to go on for?"

"Several months"

"What did you do with your old map?"

I rolled that up and put it in my chest months ago. My tablet took the place of that old map, it's a bit getting used to. You should just give it to me I'll teach you how to use it.

"Have you thought about retiring?"

"Yes," I have.

Suddenly something rocked the submarine, hold on. With that the Commander quickly stood up and walked down to the Command Center. He walked over to the sailor that was monitoring the sonar, and the sailor looked up at him.

"What are you seeing on the sonar?"

"A drone ship."

"It's an enemy vessel, we must do something."

"What's our plan for attack?"

"We'll fire an anti-drone ship missile."

A newly transformed zombie sailor was lumbering towards the Commander, without letting anyone else know he quickly pulled out his gun and shot the zombie in the head. That just took us all by surprise, it surprises me that you would shoot one of your own men. What was I supposed to do he had changed into a zombie; I wasn't going to let him eat me. A week later the Commander and his crew had abandoned the submarine after it sustained massive damage from a torpedo from an enemy vessel and swam to safety onto an island where they were rescued a week later.

Back in London Loraine and Douglas were driving in their Land Rover, with half a tank of gas. Loraine was sick to her stomach, and had a bad headache. Douglas was driving at a high rate of speed down the bridge that led out of London.

Douglass knows London better than most people and he knew of a castle that was two hours away from where they were. He wasn't sure if the castle was going to be overrun by zombies, I think that you better slow down dear.

"What for?"

"You might hit a stopped car or run into a zombie."

"Do you see any zombies around here?"

"No"

You never know when a zombie may appear, I'll slow down. Douglass slowed down to forty-five miles per hour, we're going to have to pull over.

"Why"

"I can see that the oil light is lit up on the dash."

We've almost run out of oil, once we do the engine will overheat and we'll be stranded in the middle of nowhere with these crazy zombies. I'll pull off the road for a short while before we have to go again. Suddenly they heard an explosion nearby.

"What was that?"

"I don't know, I'll get out and check."

Please be careful baby, I will be don't worry.

"Why don't you take your gun with you?"

"That's a good idea"

"Do you have extra bullets with you?"

"Yes," I do

I have my gun with me baby, and it's ready to go. That's my girl,
Douglass slammed the door, and walked around to the front of his truck.
He happened to look down and noticed that the front tire had blown out
and was now down to the rim. The other tires seemed to be losing air,
he quickly got back in the truck.

Loraine looked him in the eyes and asked him what's the matter with the
truck. Here's the bad news, go ahead and tell me. The one front tire
blew out and the other tires are losing air, we're going to have to walk
the rest of the way.

"How far are we going to have to walk?"

"I don't know but we have plenty of fire power to keep
the zombies away, I don't think so."

"Why not?"

"What if there's too many of them?"

"There won't be too many."

"How do you know?"

"We aren't in the city and there aren't too many
zombies wandering around the outskirts of the city."

"What are you now the zombie forecaster?"

"No," I'm not

Let's stop wasting time here and get walking, I don't have all the stuff ready. You better get everything ready now, I just heard something groan, it's probably a zombie. Don't worry baby I'll protect you from these zombies.

That's true but, once one zombie shows up then more will show up. All the zombies want to do is to attack and kill you. They're no longer considered to be human, I know that you don't have to explain that to me.

"Do you have the extra ammunition with you?"

"Yes," I just put the extra ammunition in my back pocket.

"How many bullets?"

"I don't know, I didn't take the time to count the bullets."

I'm ready to fight off some zombies, I hate leaving our truck here abandoned. But we have to there's no way out of the situation. Let's go, I'm ready to go. Douglass and Loraine began walking down the street towards the bridge leading out of London.

Ahead of them they could see that the road had hundreds of abandoned cars and trucks on it. They could see that there was something walking around in the middle of the street. It looked like a dog or even a leopard, as they got closer to it, it resembled a German Shepard.

The German Shepard didn't seem like it had the virus living inside of its body and was calm as they walked closer to it. He let them pet him on the head. What a good dog its ashame that this dog was let go. They heard a loud growl, coming from nearby.

They looked over and saw a few zombies lumbering around, the zombies looked confused. One of the three zombies was missing his arm and his leg was missing. Blood was running from his eyes and mouth, his white shirt was all stained with blood.

The zombie off to the left of him was missing both arms and was barely able to balance anymore. He fell down and began to pull himself along on the ground. He barely could move along, Loraine took her gun out of the holster and shot the crawling zombie right in the head.

His head exploded and he stopped moving. While the two other zombies began to run after them, the one zombie ran up a few feet away from her.

Loraine shot and the bullet hit him in the head causing him to collapse. The final zombie approached, and Douglass pulled out his gun and took a precise shot hitting the last zombie in the head and watched his body fall to the ground.

There was a large tractor trailer truck and there was no one in it, along the side of the truck it said fresh poultry and farm fresh products. Him and Loraine slowly walked around towards the back of the truck. They knew that something bad might happen and more zombies would come out of hiding.

Loraine went first and peeked around the corner, what she saw absolutely made her terrified. There were several zombies sitting down eating chickens, the zombies were so interested in eating the chickens they didn't notice them at first.

Loraine happened to look down and saw that there was crow bar lying by her foot. The doors to the trailer were metal doors and the doors looked to be in good shape. Two of the zombies that were in the back of the truck were lying down and eating while the rest of them were sitting up to eat.

One of the zombies had blood running out of his mouth and he made a groaning sound and kept on eating the chicken. The zombies seemed like they were confused, one of the zombies was shaking his arm and groaning. Then one of the zombies put down the chicken and looked over in Loraine's direction.

Loraine was immediately horrified and she shook her head, I need help when I tell you to grab the crowbar help me to wedge it in-between the trailer doors.

"Why do you want to do that?"

"There are several zombies in there waiting to jump out and attack us."

"So will you help me right now?"

"Yes"

Douglass took one look in the trailer and bent down and picked up the crow bar. He quickly wedged it in the door, and when he did he could hear that zombies were trying to break open the door. They heard one loud slam, followed by a low growl. Look out, there's a zombie a few feet away from us.

"How comes the zombie has his head up in the air sniffing?"

"He probably smells us and wants to have us for dinner if you don't shoot him."

Suddenly the zombies growled and looked Douglass right in the eyes, I think that this zombie wants to attack me. You know what to do, pull out your gun and shoot him in the head. Don't just stare at him, he's so ugly that he's making me sick. Loraine gave Douglass a hard push, too his left shoulder.

"What was that for?"

"I'm trying to make you get ready to shoot him."

I don't want to waste another bullet besides that, there's an old shovel right here underneath this old car sitting here. Then kill him with the shovel.

Quickly honey, the zombie came lumbering over and let out a great groan, and he was now within striking range of the shovel. Douglass swung the shovel once and struck the zombie on the left side of his head.

The zombie collapsed onto the ground and began to crawl towards him. He once again swung the shovel and hit him again in the head at the same place. The zombie let out a growl and kept on crawling closer to Douglass. Look out the zombie is going to bit your leg, he's not.

He swung the shovel one last time and this time after hitting the zombie on the head for a third time, this time the zombie stopped moving and laid there motionless.

I didn't think that zombie was ever going to die, he just kept on trying to get me. I know, zombies aren't your friend that's for sure. Let's move on, you know I don't think it was a good idea for us to walk across this bridge.

"Why not?"

"There are too many zombies and I don't want to get bitten and become one."

"Why would you even think that way?"

"I don't know"

You and me should split up and that would help us to move along much quicker. Were in this situation together and there's no turning back now.

"Are you afraid of the zombies?"

"Yes," I am

I wouldn't been able to get this far without you, that's why I love you so much.

"What was that?"

"I don't know, it sounded like a loud explosion."

It's coming from somewhere in the city, I just saw an explosion over there in the city. Suddenly a large military helicopter flew over the bridge. Let's wave our arms to get their attention, no that's not a good idea.

What if they mistake us as zombies and shoot us, you know what you're so scared and don't want to say it. I'm not scared, but I want to get out of here. Look the helicopter just swooped in closer to the bridge and is just hovering there. I wander what they're doing over there.

"How about we go find out?"

"No," thanks I'm good right where I'm at.

"Where's your adventurous spirit?"

"I don't have a spirit or any of that."

"Just please be careful if you go look."

I don't want you to fall off of the bridge and get hurt, I'm not going to get hurt, I can handle myself just fine. It's you, you talk too much the whole day is going to be over by the time you stop talking.

I didn't make this mess, the government did, I even bet that the government is listening to us arguing and laughing at us. Don't say that, you're talking like you have lost your mind.

Suddenly the bridge shook and eight zombies came running out of hiding and tried to jump up at the helicopter, the pilot immediately unloaded so much fire power that the zombies were killed instantly. Then it grew eerily quiet, once the dust had settled. There's an abandoned bank truck.

"Do you think that there's any money in it?"

"No," I highly doubt it.

"You're such a doubting Thomas today."

"What has gotten into you?"

"I'm just upset about what is going on."

You might as well get over it, because things aren't going to get a whole lot better for you and me. Were stuck in a world of the undead and I'm not happy about it.

We could have crossed the bridge by now and have reached the castle before sun down. It's too dangerous to stay out after dark, don't worry about how you don't have a life. We're going to have a good life together, now don't you forget that. I just looked in the window of the bank truck and there's a dead man sitting on the passenger seat.

Thank goodness the doors look to be locked, for I'm not in the mood to have to shoot another dumb dead guy. The back of the bank truck is open. Don't leave it open, and Loraine slammed the door shut.

We have to be quiet, I don't want any more zombies to come out and annoy us. I can't stand seeing dumb dead mindless people walking around.

"Why don't we run instead of walk?"

"No," then I'll get tired.

Come on you lazy bones, let's you and I run. I'll race you, no thanks.

"If I hold your hand would you run with me?"

"Yes," I will.

Douglas and Loraine began to run and they ran in and out of the lines of abandoned cars and trucks, suddenly Loraine stopped running and froze.

"What's the matter baby?"

"Didn't you see that?"

"See what?"

"I just saw a giant walk zombie walk by."

"How tall was he?"

"He looked like he was almost seven feet tall."

Chapter Two: Survivors Reunited

We don't want him to see us, that's for sure, a month before the outbreak I read a book about giants, it was titled "Giants Among Us." It said that the giants died out two-hundred years ago, but it did say that scientist tried to bring them back to life, recently.

It probably escaped the laboratory, and is now terrorizing everything around it. Let's get a move on. That giant zombie really scared me, I'm ready to get into the castle. Look over there, at the castle. It looks like the castle was under attack.

The helicopter is back, maybe the helicopter is trying to kill the giant zombie. That's what it seems like, I think that the zombie is going to get killed by the helicopter.

"Don't you?"

"Yes," I hope so

Don't get tired on me now, let's go on until we reach the castle. I smell a foul odor in the air, it smells of rotting flesh and rotten eggs; I can't stand it.

A fighter jet flew overhead, and explosions ensued. I don't like the fact that the fighter jets are targeting zombies so close to us, I'm glad that they're protecting us but I don't want to be blown up. I wonder how many zombies they have blown up by now, I'd say thousands of them.

I wish that we were hiding in a bunker somewhere, I liked walking down the streets before and greeting friends and now I don't care if I don't walk on a street ever again. Several rats darted out in front of them, I'm getting tired of stepping over dead rats.

"How many fighter jets do you think are flying around here?"

"Ten"

I don't care which one of us is stronger, let's keep our differences aside. Look behind you, the bridge got struck by an incoming missile and collapsed into the water below.

"Do you even care about the bridge falling down?"

"No," I don't care

Look in front of us, it's the castle. We have reached it at last, but now we have a whole new problem.

"What's that?"

"I can't get the door to open and there's a large metal lock on the front door of the place."

Let's not give up that easily, I'm sure that there's another way to get into the castle, perhaps there's a back door. That's wishful thinking, but I don't think that they want us to get in. That's not true, I'm almost out of breath, and are so tired. The helicopter just shot another missile into the bridge knocking the rest of it over.

Look there's that giant zombie, where point him out to me. You see that one part of the bridge is still standing, yes now look all the way over to your left and tell me when you see him. Now I do, look at him, he must be a mutant or something like that. I'd like to know where he comes from.

"Why's that?"

"I've never saw a person that was so big as he is."

It seems to me that he's trying to escape the constant bombardment. He just tried to jump but lost his footing and fell into the water. The giant zombie looks like he's trying to swim.

He's a dumb zombie and is going to sink to the bottom of the blackish trash filled ocean. Let's stop sitting here and get a move on. Hey now you're telling me what to do, and you aren't letting me rest.

I'm a women and need more rest then you, I hope you don't think that way. You're really getting on my nerves. You have been bothering me all day, so they both carefully walked around the back of the castle. There's a problem, I just accidentally dropped my extra clip, and two bullets fell out of it.

"Would you help me to pick them up?"

"No," pick them up yourself

I'll try to find a way in while you do that, I see how it is. Stop belly aching and pick up the bullets. Loraine walked on and saw there were some green vines growing over the side of the castle.

There was a small door that a person could barely fit through. The door had a large silver metal lock, the door know was all tarnished and was beginning to rust.

She walked around the other side and saw a bunny rabbit and thought to herself this is odd, it must be some type of trap or something. Suddenly three zombies came running towards the bunny and they were too slow to catch the bunny.

The three zombies moaned and groaned and one of them growled as it looked over at Loraine. Loraine yelled out let me in. The zombies heard her and began lumbering along towards her. You zombies aren't going to get me, but I'm going to get you. Stand back you mindless corpses and feel my wrath.

Loraine pulled out her pistol and shot the three zombies in the head and their heads exploded and made blood splatter all over the wall of the castle. See that, I'm not a zombie, I'll kill them so you should let me in your castle. Suddenly the one window slid down and an old decrepit man looked out.

"What do you want Ma'am?"

"I want to come in"

"Are you infected?"

"No"

"Do I look infested to you?"

"No," so come on in.

"What's your name?"

"My name is Loraine"

"Is there anyone else with you today?"

"Yes," my boyfriend Douglass is still out there.

"What's he doing?"

"He dropped his stuff and is picking it up."

He should be coming over here shortly. Here he comes, so what's your name old fellow. My name is Bart.

"How long have you been hiding in the castle for?"

"I've been here for many months."

"Who else is in here?"

"There are fifty other survivors in here."

"What do you know about the zombies?"

"I don't know much about them."

I happened to see a giant zombie, who must have been seven feet tall.

"Do you know anything about that?"

"No," I'm sorry I don't.

There's one person here that's a Russian scientist.

"What's his name?"

"It's a woman, her name is Tara."

"Do you have any weapons Bart?"

"No," I don't but Tara does.

"Do you know what kind of guns?"

"Yes," she has an assault rifle and a knife.

"Who threw the bunny outside?"

"That was me"

"Did you hear me yelling let me in?"

"Yes," I did, but I waited to see if you were infected or not.

"How could you tell that I wasn't infected?"

"We'll because I didn't see any blood coming out of your eyes."

"How many zombies have you watched go by here?"

"I've saw ten zombies today"

"Did you see"

"What happened to the bridge?"

"Yes," I was watching the bridge fall down.

"Has any zombies gotten in here?"

"Just one and Tara killed the zombie."

"Do you see more women zombies than men zombies?"

"I've seen about the same amount."

Yesterday I saw a rabid zombie dog

"What do they look like?"

"Oh just a regular dog but blood is running out of their mouth, and their eyes are red."

"Do the zombie dogs attack the zombie people?"

"Yes," they do.

"What happens here when it gets dark?"

"Not much I just sleep and don't go outside."

There's a zombie dog that lives near hear and he howls sometimes at midnight.

"Does that annoy you?"

"No"

I'm just glad to be in here, and safe.

"Where's your family?"

"They're gone."

"They turned into zombies and I had to run away from them."

"How did they become zombies?"

"They got bit by a little boy zombie, who they thought wasn't infected."

"How many kids did you have?"

"I had two kids, who I loved very much."

"All is lost now, I'm not happy to be here."

"Have you talked to Tara today?"

"Yes," I have and she wants nothing to do with me

"How do know that?"

"She told me."

"Are you comfortable sitting in that old rocking chair?"

"Yes"

I'm about ready to fall asleep, suddenly the ground shook what was that? I don't know it could have been an earthquake.

"What if it was a bomb going off?"

"No," it wasn't a bomb

"Why would you even say that?"

"It was just a guess."

"What do you have to eat here?"

"We have cereal and other kinds of food."

"Why would you ask him that for?"

"I was just curious."

I can tell that you're still in a bad mood. I'm getting hungry, do you have some cereal I could have? Hold on, I have to go out to the pantry.

"Where's the pantry?"

"It's upstairs in the eating area."

"How about if you come with me?"

"Go ahead honey, I'll wait here."

I might take a nap, while you're gone. I've never heard of the eating area being upstairs, it's upstairs because of the zombies.

"Have you had a zombie problem?"

"Yes"

"When did that happen?"

"About a week ago."

"How did you stop them"

"By shooting them"

"Do you usually talk this much?"

"No"

I'm just glad to see you and be able to talk to you.

"How are you feeling right now?"

"Bart replied I'm getting tired, it's going on six o clock and I'm ready to go back to sleep."

"What time do you go to bed?"

"I go to bed at eight o clock"

"How many steps do we have to climb up?"

"Another five six steps."

This castle has too many steps, I know how you feel, and I feel the same way. I hate steps but there is no elevator. On the good side walking up all these steps can help you to lose weight.

"Are you trying to lose weight?"

"No," and I don't plan to.

I'm already in good shape, I'm almost out of breath, and I'm all sweaty and my knee is aching.

"Would you like a pain pill?"

"No," I'll be okay

Wow there's a lot of room up here

"How many people come up here during the day?"

"Not many, we all eat at six o clock."

We had pizza and garlic bread, that sounds good.

"Do you have any leftover pizza?"

"I'm not sure, I'll check on that"

"Do you have a chef here?"

"No," we don't

I would rather cook my own food and not let anyone else cook.

"Where do you get the food from?"

"We get it from the downtown grocery store."

"Who goes on the supply runs?"

"Our security team"

"How many people are in it?"

"Six of them"

I don't feel like answering any more of your questions, I need some quiet time. One last question.

"How many children are here?"

"There are five kids that we rescued."

Chapter Three: Settling In

I don't feel like telling you how we saved them, the story is too long to tell. I'm tired of talking and want to lay down soon, I'm sorry if I upset you, no we didn't upset me. Bart opened the pantry door, and Douglass looked in it and there was a big box of cereal.

"Would you mind if I took the box of cereal down stairs with me?"

"No"

Don't go outside of the castle while you are eating or the zombies may attack you. A man yesterday went outside of the castle and was eating a chicken sandwich and he got mauled by the zombies and expected me to let him back in.

He turned into a zombie just an hour later after being mauled, the first thing that happened to him was he began to bleed from his eyes then he began to growl at me. I didn't leave him back him, but left him outside. He must have been hungry still and began to attack another zombie who was just walking by.

He ran over to the other zombie and ripped off his arm and began to gnawing on the decapitated arm. I haven't saw him again after that day, be careful walking down the steps, the stairs are steep and I already twisted my ankle on the stairs and let me tell you it really hurts and I don't want to ever do it again.

        "Have you ever twisted your ankles?"

        "No"

I'm careful when I'm walking down steep steps, I like the stone steps, they look unique.

        "Do you know who the owner of this castle is?"

        "No"

Once at the bottom of the steps, Douglass looked over at and she looked back at him. There's not much variety, to eat around here, so I figured that I would bring you a box of cereal

Is the box full because I'm feeling very hungry. I don't know if the box is full, but I'm going to check. Let me reach my hand in the box and check. It's about half full, that's alright. I love cereal, and can't get enough of it.

"Douglass asked where did Bart go?"

"He's tired and went into another room to lay down."

"How's he acting?"

"He's on the grumpy side and told me to stop asking him so many questions."

I didn't think I asked him an overly amount of questions. You shouldn't upset him, after all he was the one that let us in here so I don't want him to kick us out. He's not going to kick us out don't worry.

He's a good guy; you're talking like you have known him for years. You just met him a few hours ago, and you must be careful. Suddenly you think you're the one in charge here. That's enough, I wasn't talking ugly to you.

"Why must you start an argument with me now?"

"I'm just in a bad mood"

Then you can go into another room for a while and sit alone if you're going to yell at me. I'm done arguing with you, I love to sit with you and you know that. Then sit down with me, and try to relax.

"Is Bart coming back in here to chat again?"

"No," I just said that he's tired and wants to rest.

I thought that he was going to, show me where Tara was. he forgot, or maybe he got busy, I see that you're munching, away.

"How's the cereal?"

"It tastes stale, then stop eating it."

Then what am I going to eat besides the cereal? I don't know, and I don't feel like walking up the seven or eight steps to get up into the kitchen.

"Why don't you go up there and take a look for yourself?"

"I think that I will."

Since Bart and you're acting like grumpy old men, you should spend time together. Loraine slowly went up the steps. While Douglas stood up and walked out towards a room he wasn't familiar with.

The room was dark and he couldn't see what was in the room. He walked over towards the darkened room and almost tripped over, an end table or a couch. There was an old lamp, sitting on the end table.

There was an old worn out rug on the floor, in front of the end table. There were two old lights hanging from the ceiling, both the lights were turned off and the one light bulb was broke. In the middle of the room was an old pool table, the pool table had dust all over the top of it. There were no balls on the table top.

There was an old bar stool, and the leather, was beginning to fall off. Douglass didn't want to touch the bar stool, he stepped on something and bent down and took a look, it was a green tennis ball. There was a broken pool que lying on top of the pool table.

There was an old brown shelf hanging on the wall, by the entrance of the room. There was old wallpaper lining the room, the ugly greenish brown color, the room was cool and he got a chill that ran all the way down his back. He shook off the chill and continued on walking back towards the very back of the room.

There was a leather chair, in his path and he walked around it and ended up tripping over another rug. When he fell his chin hit the leather chair and his knee got twisted and he let out an ouch. As he was getting back up a black cat came walking over and tried to jump up on him.

You silly cat get off of me, I hate cats and please get off. The black cat remained on his shoulder, this is the last time that I'm going to tell you to get off, I can tell that were going to be the best of friends and he grabbed the cat by its legs, and threw him out in front of him and he bounced off of the last remaining light making the light bulb shatter. The cat landed on the pool table and kept on staring at him.

Stop staring at me I did nothing to you, now leave me alone cat. Douglass thought to himself I wonder where Bart got to. He heard a loud slamming sound and wasn't sure where it was coming from. He saw that there was another room that led to somewhere he didn't know, he was curious and as he walked closer to the entrance of the next room.

He heard the slamming sound again and it seemed like he was closer to whatever was making the noise. The cat was still following behind him, look you silly cat, go back to wherever you came from and leave me alone. However, the next room he walked into was darker then the room he had just left.

There was what looked like a giant cage, but he couldn't be sure that's what it was. He saw that there was a huge metal lock on the cage. The cage was all black, and he couldn't see what was in the cage. Then he heard a low growl and a hand came reaching out around the side of the cage. Get your hand away from me you creep, Douglass backed away and was getting irritated. There was one light above the cage, he heard that someone was moaning and groaning. Suddenly the light above the cage lit, now he could clearly see what was in the cage.

There were three zombies who were in chains and two of them had gotten there chains off. The one zombie looked absolutely horrifying, he was missing his left eye and blood was running out of his mouth. The zombies stank so bad, that Douglass could barely stand it, he held his nose shut. There were flying insects all over the one zombie.

There were hundreds of flies on his back and he was missing his arm, there was a women zombie who was trying to bite the other zombie's hands. The zombies were growling and more agitated since the light was turned on. Douglass wasn't sure who turned the light on.

"Hello who's there?"

"The room went silent."

I'm only going to ask one more time.

"Who's in the room with me?"

"It's got to be you Bart."

He heard a door slam shut and Bart and Tara walked into the room.

"What are you doing in here?"

"I was just exploring"

Next time tell us what you're doing, you shouldn't be in this room.

"Why not?"

"Because we have secrets that we didn't want you and your girlfriend to find out about it."

You think it's okay to keep some zombies locked up in a cage, we think it's just fine.

"Why are the zombies in here anyway?"

"They're in here, because we have been doing experiments with them."

"May I ask what kind of experiments?"

"No," you can't

Don't wander around here again or you might get yourself killed.

"Where's your girlfriend at?"

"I don't know"

She said that she was looking for some food, this is the first and final warning that you're going to get. Next time we find you in here, we'll tazor you until you leave the room. That's so harsh, we don't want you to interrupt our work that we have been doing.

I don't understand what the big secret is here, to me these are just regular zombies that are killing machines. Exactly right, but these zombies aren't your regular zombie. See we have injected them with insect DNA.

"From what insect?"

"The fly"

"Why did you do that?"

To see if the zombies would grow wings and act like flies, that sounds in human to me.

"What gives you guys the rights to do this?"

"The government and that's enough questions for now."

"Why don't you get out of this room and go find your annoying girlfriend?"

"She's not annoying to me, you two just leave this castle."

"Are you kicking us out?"

"No," you have to leave our experiments alone.

I should of freed the zombies so that they can attack you guys, It's not right what you're doing to these zombies. They used to be people just like us. They're no longer humans but blood thirty monsters.

How do you suppose you're going to keep these zombies alive, by feeding them dogs and cats that we find wandering around on street corners. You both should be ashamed of yourselves, you don't feed dogs and cats to zombies. What are you all of a sudden the expert on what zombies should eat.

Now don't talk smart to me Bart said Douglass just be quiet, you're just making things worse for yourself. I don't like cats, but I'd never think about, feeding a cat to a zombie. You should go out and find a cow and give that to the zombies, Bart and Tara looked at each other then looked back at Douglass.

We should just tazor you and threw you in with the zombies. That's not a good idea and you would be committing murder. We don't think that anyone would miss you, if you went missing. Proceed on and leave this room now, this black cat shouldn't be given to the zombies.

Just stop talking and get out of here, they slammed the door shut and locked the door. Now stay out of this room or else, Douglass walked along and all of a sudden the floor creaked and scared him. The room was still dark and there was a planter off to his left and he almost walked into it.

There were another set of table and chairs, off to his right. The pool table seemed like it was moved, over closer to the back door, and he couldn't understand why. He just kept on walking until he reached the bottom of the steps that led to the upstairs kitchen. Loraine was nowhere to be found.

Douglass began walking up the steep steps, the steps creaked and cracked but Douglass kept on walking up the steps and it didn't take him very long to reach the top, and when he did he saw that Loraine was sitting in a blue recliner eating a bag of chips and popcorn.

"How are you doing?"

"I'm doing great since I've found some chips and popcorn."

"Couldn't you find anything else to eat?"

"Yes," I did

I found a bag of bread, but after taking a closer look at it, it had some green mold all over it. There were ants crawling out of the bread when I picked it up.

I quickly dropped the bread on the floor and stumped on it, to kill all of the ants. I can't stand even the sight of ants, he couldn't have been that bad, you didn't see all the ants that crawled out of the bread.

"Where did you throw the bread?"

"I threw the bread in the trash can"

Where were you this whole time, now don't make up a story, I know what you were doing. You don't know what I was doing, I was curious what was back there and I found out.

"What's back there?"

"You don't want to know, come on I do want to know."

There are zombies back there in cages and are being fed cats and dogs.

"That's absolutely horrific"

"In an angered voice Douglass said who does Bart think he is?"

"I don't know but they threatened me"

"How so?"

They said that they're going to taze me and throw me into the zombie cage. They are mean people and I don't know where everyone else has gone to.

I hope that they weren't killed and fed to the zombies. It wouldn't surprise me if that was the case, this castle stinks like dead stink bugs and rotting flesh. It does have a horrible odor to it, I don't mind it as much as you do.

"What else are they doing to the zombies?"

"They're doing crazy experiments and injecting them with fly DNA."

"Do you think we could stop them?"

"No"

I don't know how to fight that well, and besides that I'm tired this evening.

"Do you think I could sneak back there and let the zombies out of the cage?"

"That would be suicide, and isn't worth it."

Those zombies would be after you so fast you would never have a chance to live with them around, you don't have your gun on you.

"Why not?"

"I dropped it somewhere in the one dark room."

Chapter Four: The Trouble

You didn't take a moment and even look for your gun. That's when I found that secret room, I have my gun on me and they'll do what I want. They probably have guns more powerful than ours, they don't, I don't think that Bart has a gun or knows how to use it.

I think we should let the zombies out of the cage so they can be free to attack and kill Bart and Tara. I don't want to see them killed or mauled by zombies.

Why not, they're mean people. How about you check and make sure that they are fast asleep tonight and I'll let the zombies out tonight and then we'll leave this castle and find shelter somewhere else. I don't of any other castles or places to hide from the scary outside world.

I'm sure that we could find another place to hide in, I don't like how Bart is acting like Hitler and trying to keep us here. He's a mean man and so is Tara, I think she has more problems than he does.

You know what else, Tara stinks like body odor and leaves her hair a complete mess. I don't who Bart thinks he's walking around here ruling over us. He should be glad he has a castle to hide in, that's exactly what I was thinking.

"So do you want to do what we just talked about tonight?"

"Yes," it sounds good to me

A door opened and Tara and Bart walked into the room.

"How are you two doing?"

"We're doing fine and dandy"

"What do you two want from us?"

We don't want anything from you guys, I Just wanted to see how you were doing.

"Do you have any candles or something that smells good to burn around here?"

"No"

It smells like dead stink bugs and rotten eggs in this castle, we can't help that. Were now going to go to sleep, so we'll see the both of you bright and early tomorrow.

Don't let your boyfriend walk around the rest of the castle. He has gotten himself into a lot of trouble, around here with us. Even though we will be sleeping it doesn't mean that you two can walk around in here.

"Who says?"

"I do, and don't you forget it"

I would watch what you say Tara, Loraine pulled out her forty-five pistol and pointed it right at Tara and Bart. The both of you're going to listen to me, you don't even have that gun loaded. You can't scare us, but nice try. I'll shoot, I'll prove it. Or I'll keep laughing in your face. Loraine accidentally squeezed the trigger and the gun went off. A bullet hit Tara in her chest, knocking her down onto the floor. Blood quickly began to pour out of the hole in her chest, Tara went limp and was barely breathing. Bart looked over at Loraine.

"What have you done?"

"Tara was a nice woman, no she wasn't, I can't believe you."

You shot and killed someone that I love, you didn't love her, yes I did and now I want you two to get out of my castle. Douglass replied this castle doesn't belong to you and you're a tyrant.

I don't care what you two have to say, Loraine held up her gun again and squeezed the trigger and fired it right at Bart. The bullet struck him in the chest, making him fall back onto the floor.

"How do you feel now?"

"There was there answer and Loraine realized that he was dead."

You really did it now, I think that we better get out of here, I feel just fine here. Let's get out of here, I just heard a loud banging sound I don't know what it was, but I'm scared. I hope the zombies didn't escape out of their cage.

I bet they did, then a loud moaning sound came out of one of the darkened rooms. I think we need to go upstairs and lock the door behind us. I think that's a good idea, let's go then.

"Do you still have your gun with you asked Lorraine?"

"Yes," I do but it just has two bullets left.

"How about your gun?"

"What about it?"

"Do you have enough bullets?"

"I have plenty of bullets"

It's taking us forever just to get to the top of the steps, I know but we have to do what we have to do to get away. I have almost worked up a sweat from these steps.

"How about you?"

"I'm just fine and that means that you're too out of shape."

Would you stop picking on me, I never will as long as we are together. Now that we have reached the top floor of the castle, what do you think we should do? We should look for a window or another way out of here.

Don't look through the kitchen, but I'm hungry again. I don't care how hungry you get. Let's keep on going, the zombies aren't going to stop marching on unless we shoot them. The zombies don't take any breaks; they march on no matter what.

I think that you are beginning to go out of your mind. I'm not far from it, that's for sure. Please help me to find a hatch that leads to the roof of the castle.

I can't see that well in here, we need to look for a flashlight. You actually think there's a flashlight in here. Yes, I think there has to be an old flashlight in here. Your eyes will adjust to the darkness, my eye sight isn't as good as yours.

"Why are you reaching around over there?"

"I'm looking for a secret hatch."

"What does a secret hatch look like?"

"It's just a handle that opens up a hidden door."

"Is that a trapped door?"

"Yes"

Just from touching the wall, my fingers are now black. The walls of this castle are so dirty and I'm tired of these zombies chasing us. You and I are going to get through this. How If we can't even find a way out, Then suddenly they heard a loud slam and the door began to creak. I think the zombies are almost through the door at the bottom of the steps. Yes, I believe you

"Can I hide behind you?"

"No," stay standing my right side.

Once the zombies are through the door, we'll have to start shooting and taking them out.

"What was that flying around?"

"I don't know, I didn't see it."

I'm too focused on looking for a hatch to get us onto the roof of the castle. Something just landed on my shoulder, and it's all black and has wings. It's a bat and I hate bats.

"What should I do?"

"Just stay still and leave the bat alone"

The bat is perched on my shoulder, and I'm so nervous that I'm getting all sweaty. It's just a stupid bat, here I'll get him off of your shoulder.

The one light above us is beginning to flicker, and it's scaring me. I feel like I'm in a spook house.

You're so dramatic we have bigger fish to fry then some goofy bat. Douglass pushed the bat off of Loraine's shoulder, thank you so much for doing that.

Please continue to look a handle. I see one, but it looks like it may be rusted shut. It better not be, here step aside, and let me at it. Douglass grabbed a hold of the rusted handle and pulled as hard as he could and it came open. It must have been windy outside and some cold air blew in and made him get goose bumps all over his hairy arms.

"What's the matter?"

"Some cold air blew up in my face and gave me the chills."

Hurry up there's a zombie slowly walking up the steps, the zombie has flies all over the left side of his face. I'm going to shoot him, go ahead you don't need to tell me. I was just trying to be considerate to you that's all.

Loraine's hands were shaking and she was having great difficulty getting a good aim on the zombie. I can't seem to stay still and my arms and hands won't stop shaking.

"Do you want me to shoot the zombie for you?"

"Yes," I do please

Quick hand me the pistol, Douglas aimed and fired hitting the zombie right between the eyes. Good shot honey, thank you. Wait there comes another zombie, this zombie has grown wings, and is trying to fly. Just quick shoot him now.

Hold on, let me aim and I will shoot him. Once again he aimed and shot the zombie right between the eyes. That was another good shot, he should think about climbing out of the window and getting onto the roof. It's no longer safe in here anymore, let's go now, come on climb out through the secret door out to the roof.

"Am I going to have carry you out of here?"

"No"

Then three zombies were trying to grab a hold of, but she was able to escape. Shoot them, I'm trying but my pistol just jammed. We need to look for a safe way off of the roof, it's a far drop from up here to down there.

We have to find a way or the zombies are going to get us, can't you see those three zombies trying to get out the window to get us. Yes, I do and I'm so scared right now.

"How's your gun doing?"

"It's still jammed."

Forget about my gun right now, we need to get off the roof and soon. Besides that, it's beginning to rain and pretty soon this roof is going to get slipperily and we stand a good change of slipping off the roof and breaking our legs.

We're not going to break our legs, did you look down and realize that our bones will snap if we fall down there. It must be a sixty foot drop, no I don't think so.

Stop arguing with me and find a way off this roof, I may have found a way off the roof. There's a telephone pole, leaning over and there are some thick wires that he could hold on to slow down our decent. That's a good idea but look, there's a zombie dog down there just waiting for us.

Can't you get your gun unjammed, I can't and I'm done trying to fix this gun, it's ruined and I can't fix it. I'm going to throw the gun down off of the roof. I'm going to throw it at the zombie dog and see if we still knows how to play fetch. Don't talk so stupid. I don't want you to throw your gun at him.

> "Why not?"

> "We're going to have to kill him before we get off of this roof."

> "Where's your gun?"

> "It's right here in my purse."

Get it out and let's shoot the zombie dog before we get down there. Are you sure those wires that are exposed on the telephone pole aren't going to shock us. No, I don't think so and I don't think the power grid is still functioning anyway.

Listen this is the only way I see of us being able to get off of the roof. If you have a better idea of how were going to get off of this roof, I would like to hear it. I don't that's what I thought that you would say.

"Could you please pass your gun to me?"

"It makes no sense for us to keep standing up here and getting soaked because of the rainstorm that's right over our heads."

We need to make a move now; you know your hand is shaking yes I know that.

"How many bullets do you have left in the gun?"

"Three bullets"

No, that's not good enough, you can't guess how many bullets you have, you must know exactly how many there are. Would you stop picking on me, I'm just trying get by here and you want to worry about bullets. Without guns we would have been dead a long time ago, now pull the clip out and count the bullets. The gun is getting slipperily from the rain.

I see a change in you, it's not for the greater good. There are several bullets in the clip. That's plenty, hurry up and aim at the zombie dog, what do you think I'm trying to do.

"Are you going to make a head shot?"

"I don't know if I'm a good enough shot to do that."

Chapter Five: On Their Own

I was going to shoot the zombie dog in its back, that'll just make the dog angry. You should shoot him in the head, wish me luck. Douglass looked down the fixed sights and aimed right for the head of the dog.

The bullet struck the dog fight in the head, it fell down and laid there in a puddle of its own blood. You made a good shot, that dog won't be bothering us again anytime soon.

"Are you ready now to get off of the roof?"

"Yes," I am

I'm more than ready to get off of this roof, hold on I can feel my feet slipping from beneath me. I feel like I'm going to fall down, please take me by the arm and hold me up.

I might fall if you don't hold me up, Douglass grabbed Loraine by her left arm and they slowly walked along the roof. My hair's all soaked and so is my shirt.

"Aren't you drenched too?"

"Yes," I am

I'm out here in the rain too, I'm so scared to climb down the telephone pole. Just don't think about it, and let's go. I wish that you could hold on to me while we go down the pole.

You go first, then I'll go next. Loraine quickly slid her way down the telephone pole. She was able to get down to street level once again, She walked backwards to look up and stepped in a puddle of the dog's blood.

The dogs body was still twitching and looked like he was still alive. Loraine jumped back and fell onto her back, she quickly got back up and ran towards a parked car, she climbed up on top of the car and waited there until Douglass came down off of the pole.

"What are you doing all the way down the street?"

"The body of the dead dog twitched and scared me to death."

I thought that was still alive. He's dead, I can prove it to you. Come on get down here, Douglass climbed down off of the pole and onto the street below.

Where are we going to go next from here, I don't know that yet. You better think and fast, we need to find shelter from the rain storm. Were both drenched to the bone here.

"Why don't we see if this car were standing next to is
open?"

"It's open but this car belonged to someone else, and I
don't like to steal."

I didn't know that you liked to steal cars, I don't, but we need this car to
get around and for our protection.

"Do you know how to rewire a car?"

"Yes," I'm not the best at it.

"Where did you practice wiring a car before?"

"At my friend's garage."

If we get in the car now were going to get the seats soaked and ruin
them, good thinking. We don't have any towels or to dry off with. So
let's just climb in the car and lock the doors before any zombies come
wandering along.

"Did you know that this is a smart car?"

"No"

I can't believe that you chose to take this car, this car is terribly small
and my knees are getting crushed as I get in the driver's seat. I feel like
I'm getting crushed into a tin can, just be glad that were no longer
getting rained on. Here comes a mob of zombies.

"How many are there?"

"Too many to count"

How many is that, six, maybe seven of them. That's far too many, for us to handle. Play with the wires some more and get the car started, I'm trying, these zombies are going to get us, they're moving so slowly but soon they will be right in front of us. I just got a shock, I got it.

"Did it start?"

"Yes," it did.

"Thank goodness, so now I know you aren't just a pretty face."

Put the car in reverse and let's get out of here, Douglas threw the car in reverse and drove forward. Were almost out of here, we just missed those zombies, I'm glad that they didn't get us.

"Where to asked Douglass?"

"I don't know"

I thought that you knew where you wanted to go. Why don't we try to head out of the city and go up to the mountain and look for a cabin there. Like there's going to be a cabin on the mountain, it's so hard for me to avoid these cars that are parked all over the road.

"Would you like to drive?"

"No," because you're giving me a look like you aren't happy with my driving.

I've been driving for many years and this is definitely not my first rodeo. I love to drive and I will get us out of here safely.

"How much further until were out of the city?"

"I don't know"

I'll have to keep my eyes open for a road sign telling me how much further we need to go yet.

"What was that?"

"I heard a loud banging sound that came from the back of the car."

I can no longer control the car, it's almost impossible to steer. I'm going all over the road, you need to slow down or were going to crash and burn. I know that, what do you think I'm trying to do. You're still going forty-two miles per hour; we need to stop before we crash into another car that's on the road.

"Don't you trust my driving?"

"No," at this point I don't

Why do you have to put me down now, I've saved you from multiple zombie attacks and this is the thanks I get. I'm just in a bad mood at the moment because I'm scared.

I don't want to hear any more excuses, just say you're sorry and that's all you need to say to me. I'm sorry I talked to you in such a rude manner.

"Do you forgive me now?"

"Yes," I do.

Focus on the road with me or you can get in the back and leave everything up to me, there's no back seat in a smart car. You must keep on paying attention.

The sky looks so ugly up there, I thought that it would have stopped raining an hour ago. It's not going to stop raining now stop worrying about the weather and let's keep a look out for zombies.

"Do I have to drive and look for zombies all at the same time?"

"No," I'll help you

I'm getting hungry for a hamburger and fries; we aren't going to look for food while were in the middle of this zombie apocalypse. You don't want me to go hungry, or I might bite you. Don't kid around like that with me.

The car stopped and the steering no longer works, we're going to have to get out now and walk the rest of the way. We just got dried off and have to go out in the drenching rain again. Yes, I don't mind getting soaked again to stay alive.

"What would you rather do?"

"Stay here in the dry car and get eaten by a mob of zombies or get wet and live?"

"I'd rather live."

Were almost near the cabin, I doubt that, I bet you don't even know how much further from here the cabin is. I do know, suddenly you know where everything is, stop talking so smart to me. I had enough of your smart talk.

"What are you waiting for?"

"I'm getting out now."

"Why are you staring?"

"I'm tired and need to rest soon."

"How soon do you need to rest?"

"Twenty minutes"

"You're acting like an old man that didn't take a nap."

I'm no old man just to let you know, you're a woman who likes to complain and drive me crazy. It's easy to drive you crazy, no it's not and you know it. You're why my nerves are shot, were near the woods, and I'm afraid of the woods.

> "Why are you afraid of the woods now?"

> "There could be a mob of zombies hiding in the woods"

They could eat us while were still alive, I don't think that's going to happen. You're being so negative and I can't stand negativity. I'm getting tired of your talking.

Could you please be quiet, I'm getting drenched and I can't stand the rain. Just keep on walking along with me, then we'll find a way to the cabin. I can hear something over there between those large trees.

> "What did it sound like?"

> "Like something was walking along and breaking sticks."

> "Does it sound like it is close to us?"

> "I think it would be like eighty yards away."

I just heard a gunshot, I did too. That gunshot sounded close, we better walk faster and get out of here. Were in danger once again, there are two zombies slowly walking along over there by the trees. One of the zombies is missing his entire jaw and the zombie next to him is missing his entire arm.

"Could you please do something?"

"Do what?"

"Shoot those zombies"

I'll get right on that dear, quick before the zombies get to us. I don't think that the zombies saw us. Take a shot at those zombies, I'm begging you, just let me take a shot at them and don't hurry me. You're waiting too long. Give me the gun or else, here's the gun.

"Are you going to show me how it's done?"

"Yes"

Take the shot, quickly now they're getting closer. Loraine shot at the one zombie and hit him right in the forehead. He fell down and when he did the other zombie began to eat the dead zombie. The live zombie is feeding on the dead zombie.

He must have been very hungry like me, that's not funny, shoot that zombie and let's go. Loraine took aim and hit the second zombie in the forehead, his body fell down a small embankment. We need to go further into the woods.

"Why?"

"So that we can find the cabin before more zombies find us."

The quicker we can find the cabin the quicker we can get out of this annoying drenching rain, my hair is all soaked and is going everywhere. My scalp won't stop itching, and it's driving me absolutely crazy.

I have heard enough from you, we need to both focus our attention on finding the cabin. I do know where the cabin is, but we should it be at it soon.

"Do you think that front door of the cabin is going to open?"

"It will probably be closed and locked."

"Do you have the key to the cabin?"

"No"

I don't but we are going to find a way in, I'll try to kick in the door. I don't even think that you have the strength to kick down a door. Yes, I sure do, you never showed me that you could knock down a door.

In a few minutes I'm going to show you how to kick in a door the proper way. I didn't know that there was a proper way to kick in a door, I just figured that you would stand next to the door and give it a good kick.

"If you had to kick in a door would you?"

"No," I wouldn't

I would probably end up hurting my foot or breaking some of my toes. I see the cabin; we have finally arrived. I'm so thankful for finding the cabin.

I helped you to find the cabin, I want you to stand back and I'm going to do a back kick right into the door. Douglass began to get himself lined up with the door, and with one strong kick he was able to knock the door in.

Good job honey, you're a real tough guy. I'm going to check out the cabin, then you can come in. Douglass quickly surveyed the cabin and there were no zombies in the cabin.

It's safe for you to come in here, oh thank goodness. We should fix the front door, don't worry honey I have a plan for the door. Douglass found the right tools to repair the door.

They stayed there for a month until there was a cure discovered by a famous molecular scientist, from Poland for the infected ones and everyone was treated several weeks later. Then they moved to Delaware, and spent the rest of their days there together.

www.ingramcontent.com/pod-product-compliance
Lightning Source LLC
Chambersburg PA
CBHW081359160726
48000CB00010B/3407